Just at that moment the classroom door opened. I swung round in horror, expecting to see Miss Wise standing there, and wondering how I was going to explain to her why Charlie and I were in the classroom at lunch time with a great big bearded bloke in a bath towel.

It wasn't Miss Wise, though. If anything, it was worse.

It was Diana.

JOHN DOUGHERTY

Zeus
to the
RESCUE!

Illustrated by Georgien Overwater

YOUNG CORGI

ZEUS TO THE RESCUE!
A YOUNG CORGI BOOK 978 0 552 55372 8

Published in Great Britain by Young Corgi,
an imprint of Random House Children's Books

This edition published 2007

1 3 5 7 9 10 8 6 4 2

Copyright © John Dougherty, 2007
Illustrations copyright © Georgien Overwater, 2007

Papers used by Random House Children's Books are natural, recyclable products
made from wood grown in sustainable forests. The manufacturing processes
conform to the environmental regulations of the country of origin.

Set in 17/20pt Bembo Schoolbook
by Falcon Oast Graphic Art Ltd

Young Corgi Books are published by Random House Children's Books,
61–63 Uxbridge Road, London W5 5SA,
a division of The Random House Group Ltd,
in Australia by Random House Australia (Pty) Ltd,
20 Alfred Street, Milsons Point, Sydney, NSW 2061, Australia,
in New Zealand by Random House New Zealand Ltd,
18 Poland Road, Glenfield, Auckland 10, New Zealand,
in South Africa by Random House (Pty) Ltd,
Isle of Houghton, Corner Boundary Road & Carse O'Gowrie,
Houghton 2198, South Africa,
and in India by Random House India Pvt Ltd,
301 World Trade Tower, Hotel Intercontinental Grand Complex,
Barakhamba Lane, New Delhi 110001, India

THE RANDOM HOUSE GROUP Limited Reg. No. 954009
www.kidsatrandomhouse.co.uk

A CIP catalogue record for this book is available from the British Library.

Printed and bound in Great Britain by
Bookmarque Ltd, Croydon, Surrey

As always, with much love to
Noah & Cara

And with grateful thanks to two friends –
my classics consultant[1], Dr Vanda Zajko, and my
bovine[2] consultant, Johnny 'Nosh' Pallot[3]

---

[1] Consultant: someone you ask about things, an expert
[2] Bovine: to do with cows, cow-like
[3] When I say Johnny's my bovine consultant, I mean he knows about cows;
I don't mean he's an expert who looks like a cow . . .

Chapter One

Diana

This is me.

And this is the Greek god Zeus.

He came to stay at our house once, and caused all sorts of trouble.

This is the story of what happened when he came back.

It all started when the new girl arrived in our class.

"Put down your pencils, everyone," Miss Wise announced. "I'd like to introduce you to Diana. I'm sure you'll all make her feel at home."

Diana didn't look like she wanted to feel at home. She looked bad-tempered and a bit scary. I didn't think she was going to be very popular.

I was wrong about that. The moment Miss Wise said, "Now, who would like to sit beside Diana and look after her today?" every single girl in the class put her hand up. Every one! Even Sophie and Leah, who always sit together and never play with anyone else! It was a bit weird, to be honest.

It got weirder.

"Now, Diana," Miss Wise went on, "I'd like you to go and sit down next to Hélène, please. She'll make sure you know where everything is."

But Diana didn't sit down. Instead, she looked at Miss Wise and said, "Have you got a boyfriend?"

Everyone gasped, and held their breath. Miss Wise *hates* us being nosy.

She always says we shouldn't ask teachers personal questions, and sometimes she gets cross if we do – not shouting or anything like that, but you can just tell, which is worse in a way. Miss Wise is really nice, but you don't want to mess with her.

So we all waited to see what she would do.

And what she did was go a bit pink, and say, "No, I haven't."

"That's all right, then," Diana said, and sat down.

By playtime, it was clear that there was something very strange indeed about Diana. Although she did what Miss Wise said, she kept acting as if she was in charge – and what was stranger, Miss Wise let her. And all the girls seemed to think she was the absolute best.

"It's because she's so pretty," said Charlie as we went out to play. "Girls always like other girls if they're pretty."

"Sophie doesn't," I pointed out. "Not if they're prettier than her."

It was true. Sophie was probably the prettiest girl in the class (or had been up till that morning), and didn't she know it. She could be really mean to anyone she thought might be better-looking – but just like the others, she was fussing round Diana, trying to be her best friend.

That playtime was awful. Absolutely awful. The other girls followed Diana about as if she owned the playground – and she behaved like she did, too. She must have spoiled a dozen games in the first five minutes, barging through them as if they weren't happening. And the funny thing was, she got away with it. No one – kids or teachers – said a thing to her. There was, I thought to myself again, definitely something strange about Diana.

That was when I noticed an odd sort of feeling, a kind of tingling under my shirt. And then I realized what it was.

You see, when Zeus went away, he left me a gift – a tiny golden thunderbolt on a chain. I was wearing it, and that was what was tingling. I understood immediately.

"It's Zeus!" I whispered to Charlie.

"What is?" Charlie whispered back. He can be a bit slow on the uptake sometimes.

"Diana!" I told him. "Diana is Zeus in disguise! That's why the girls are behaving so strangely – he's done some kind of magic or something on them!"

Charlie gave me a funny look. "Don't be daft, Alex," he said. "It can't be Zeus. Zeus is a bloke! And Diana's a girl!"

I sighed. "Charlie," I reminded him, "last time Zeus was here, he turned into a hamster, a beetle and an eagle.

I don't think turning into a girl would be any harder, do you?"

"Yeah, but I bet it was a boy hamster, and a boy beetle, and a boy eagle. I mean, if he turned into a girl, what would he do with his . . . you know . . ." He went red and shuffled his feet.

I rolled my eyes. "Charlie, he's a god. I don't know what they do with their different bits when they turn into other things, but . . . oh, for goodness' sake, *look!*"

I put my hand inside my shirt and slipped the little thunderbolt out between two of the buttons. It was glowing gently.

"See?" I said.

Charlie looked unconvinced.

"Well?" he said.

"Even if it *is* Zeus, what are you going to do about it?"

"That depends," I said. "What have you brought for your playtime snack?"

Reluctantly, Charlie held up a bag of crisps. Roast beef flavour.

Zeus's favourite.

"Perfect!" I said, and grabbed them.

I waited until the bell went for lining-up, and then sidled up to Diana and held the bag out.

"Um ... would you like me to sacrifice these to you?" I asked innocently.

Diana barely seemed to notice me.

"No thanks," she said dismissively, and turned away.

Just for a second, I wondered if I might have made a mistake. But the little thunderbolt was tingling furiously now – so it *had* to be Zeus, didn't it?

"Um . . . why not?" I asked. When Zeus was here before, he'd have taken a break from *anything* for a quick sacrifice.

She looked at me again, as if she'd only just become properly aware I was there.

"Because," she said, with a sarcastic little half-smile, "you're a *boy*." The way she said it, you'd have thought it was the worst  insult in the world. "And you haven't done anything to offend me. Yet."

And then she marched up to the
front of our class line and pushed in,
right in front of Troy. The other girls
stared for a moment and then,
giggling and shouting, they ran after
her and pushed in too. Poor Troy was
elbowed and jostled further and
further down the line as they all
bumped and shoved to be next to
Diana. Of course, then he got all
upset and started yelling and trying to
get back in at the front, and the girls
wouldn't let him.

And then Miss Wise came out and
saw him, and gave him a big telling
off. It was *so* unfair – and so unlike
Miss Wise. She wouldn't listen to him at
all, just kept saying how rude it was of
him to try and push in, and how
unkind he was being to Diana on her
first day. Then she sent
him to the back. Troy
stomped down the line,
nearly in tears.

"Still think she's Zeus?"
Charlie whispered.

"No," I whispered back.

"So why's your thunderbolt glowing like that?"

"Don't know. Maybe it means I need to ask Zeus for help."

Charlie gaped at me.

"You're joking, aren't you, Alex? Remember the trouble he caused last time? You're not going to invite him back, are you?"

"Who would you rather have here causing trouble?" I asked him. "Zeus, or Diana?"

Charlie looked at Troy, who was angrily staring straight ahead and trying not to cry. Then he looked at the front of the line, where Diana, instead of waiting for Miss Wise to tell her to lead in, suddenly charged towards the door. The other girls ran after her, barging their way through the class whose turn it actually was to go.

He sighed. "What do we do, then?"

Chapter Two

On the Loose Again

At lunch time we sneaked back into the classroom.

We're not supposed to go inside without a teacher, but we had to. There was something in there that we needed.

The Temple of Zeus.

Not the real one, obviously – the model one I'd made as part of our Ancient Greek work earlier that term, which was all still on display. Although in a way it *was* a real temple, because Zeus said so. And the last time Zeus had turned up it was because someone had said a prayer into it, or one just like it.

Carefully, I picked up the model temple and began to speak into it.

"Oh, great and powerful Zeus . . ." I began.

Before I could say any more, though, the temple interrupted me.

Or at least, a voice came out of the temple – Zeus's voice. The big, booming voice he liked to use to impress people, only sounding very far away.

"GREETINGS, MORTAL," it said, making the temple quiver on its cardboard pillars.

"YOU'RE THROUGH TO MOUNT OLYMPUS. I'M AFRAID THERE'S NOBODY HERE RIGHT NOW, BUT YOUR WORSHIP *IS* IMPORTANT TO US, SO PLEASE LEAVE A PRAYER AFTER THE TONE. *BEEEEEEEEEEP!*"

Charlie looked bemused.

"I didn't think Greek gods would have an answering machine," he said.

"I don't think they do have one," I said suspiciously.

You're through to Mount Olympus

"THEY JOLLY WELL DO, YOU KNOW," said the voice.

That made me even more suspicious.

"Answering machines aren't supposed to talk back to you like that," I said.

"OH, NO?" said the voice. "THEN WHY ARE THEY CALLED ANSWERING MACHINES, IF THEY DON'T ANSWER YOU? ANSWER ME *THAT* IF YOU'RE SO SMART!"

"Because they answer the phone," I said. "Then they record a message, but they don't say anything while they're doing it."

"OH," said the voice. "WELL . . . WELL, YOU DON'T EXPECT THE GODS OF MOUNT OLYMPUS TO HAVE JUST AN *ORDINARY* ANSWERING MACHINE, DO YOU? YOU EXPECT THEM TO

HAVE A REALLY AMAZING ONE
BECAUSE THEY'RE GODS. AND
THAT'S WHAT I AM."

"What – a god?" said Charlie. He
wasn't really following this.

"YES!" said the voice. "ER . . . NO, I
MEAN. I'M A REALLY AMAZING
ANSWERING MACHINE, THAT'S
WHAT I AM. HONEST."

"Oh, come on, Zeus," I said. "I know
it's you."

"NO IT ISN'T," said the voice. "IT
ISN'T ME AT ALL. IT'S AN
ANSWERING MACHINE, MADE

telephonis

SPECIALLY FOR THE
GODS BY . . . UM . . .
TELEPHONIS, THE
GOD OF ANSWERING
MACHINES. VERY
CLEVER LIKE THAT,
TELEPHONIS IS."

"Oh, *please*, Zeus," I said.

"We really need your help." When there was no answer, I added, "I'll sacrifice a bag of crisps to you if you'll help us."

"WHAT FLAVOUR?" said the voice. "ER . . . NOT THAT I'M INTERESTED, OF COURSE. BUT *ZEUS* MIGHT BE, WHEN HE HEARS THE MESSAGE."

"Roast bull," I told him, holding the packet near the temple and crinkling it so he could hear it rustling.

"OK," said the voice. "MAKE THE SACRIFICE NOW AND I'LL . . . ER . . . *ZEUS* WILL HELP YOU LATER, WHEN HE'S GOT A MOMENT."

"No way, Zeus!" I said. "You'll get your sacrifice when I know you're going to help. Otherwise, I'm going to give the bag back to Charlie and he'll eat them."

"But . . . but . . ." the voice began, and this time it was Zeus's ordinary voice. "Oh, all right then," it went on. "Hang on a moment."

There was a funny sort of splashing sound and some muttering from the temple and then Zeus appeared beside us, dripping wet and wrapped in a huge towel. "I was in the bath," he complained. "OK, get on with it. Honestly, the things a god has to do to get a second-rate sacrifice these days."

I carefully put the
model temple on
my head – Zeus
likes me to do
that – and
opened the bag
of crisps. Zeus
took a big sniff
and grinned.

"Oh, great and
powerful Zeus," I said, "I sacrifice this
bag of roast-bull-flavour crisps to you
and ask you to do something about
this new girl who's making our lives a
misery—"

"Hang on!" Zeus interrupted. "Is
that it? A new girl? You got me out of
my nice warm bath because you're
not getting on with one of your
classmates?"

"Yeah, but there's something odd
about her," I began.

Zeus was most indignant. "I'm a god!" he said. "I'm mighty and powerful, and I used to have *loads* of worshippers! You can't summon me like a waiter just because the new kid's a bit of a weirdo!"

garçon!

I was having difficulty getting a word in edgeways. But just at that moment the classroom door opened. I swung round in horror, expecting to see Miss Wise standing there, and wondering how I was going to explain to her why Charlie and I were in the classroom at lunch time with a great big bearded bloke in a bath towel.

It wasn't Miss Wise, though. If anything, it was worse.

It was Diana.

She glared angrily.

And then she burst out: "Oh, *great*! My first day at my new school, and you turn up dressed in nothing but a towel! It's so embarrassing! How *could* you, Dad?"

My jaw dropped. "*Dad?*" I said, and looked at Zeus.

He was beaming in a slightly silly, proud sort of way. "Hello, sweetie-pie," he said.

Diana scowled even further. "*Dad!!!*"

she hissed. "How many times have I told you not to call me 'sweetie-pie' in front of mortals?"

"Sorry, poppet," Zeus said.

"*DAD?*" I said again. "You mean . . . she's your *daughter*?"

Zeus chuckled. "This," he announced proudly, "is Artemis, goddess of the moon and the hunt."

"Artemis?" Charlie said. "I thought her name was Diana!"

Diana   Artemis

"The Romans used to call her Diana," Zeus told him. "Typical of that lot; couldn't leave well enough alone. Couldn't even worship you properly without giving you a new name and pretending you'd been *their* god all along."

It was all making sense to me now.

"And she's calling herself Diana because she's in disguise, right?" I asked.

"Got it in one, Alex, kiddo." Zeus grinned. "If she's your new classmate, I can understand why you want my help!"

Diana – or Artemis – looked at me. "It's *your* fault he's here, is it?" she said. "Right, I'm turning you into a pig!"

"Hold on a moment, Artykins," Zeus said. "Alex is my High Priest. You can't turn him into a pig."

"All right, then, a goat."

"No," Zeus said.

"A hedgehog?"

"NO. Not a pig, not a goat, not a hedgehog, not anything. Think about it for a moment, Arty – how could a hedgehog make a sacrifice to me? Its paws are the wrong shape for opening the bag."

"Well, I've got to do *something* to him," Artemis said crossly. "It's his fault you're standing there in a towel embarrassing me."

"If it's the towel that's the problem," I said, "it doesn't look that different to me from what he usually wears."

Zeus grinned. "There you are, Artemis," he said, rearranging the towel so it looked like an ancient Greek tunic, only a bit fluffier.

"Problem solved."

"No, it isn't," she grumbled. "You're still here. Clear off."

Zeus's smile slipped a little. His forehead wrinkled, and little bolts of lightning flickered around it. "Artemis," he said sternly, "I may be your daddy, but I'm also king over all the gods of Mount Olympus. Tell me to clear off again and I'll spank your bottom. Anyway, I was here first."

"You never were!" Artemis said indignantly. "You've only just got here!"

"Yes, but I was here *before*, wasn't I, Sally Smartypants. Just a few weeks ago, as well you know. So maybe *you* should be the one who clears off."

Artemis scowled. "Shan't," she said, folding her arms sulkily. "It's *my* turn for a holiday, and I'm not going till I've had one. Anyway, I like it here. I've got followers, just like the old days, and my teacher hasn't got a boyfriend." She looked sternly at Zeus. "And don't go getting any ideas about that!" she said.

"I don't know *what* you mean!" Zeus said in an offended tone.

"What *does* she mean?" Charlie asked.

A little grin crept over Zeus's face.

"Well," he said, "Artemis doesn't like her followers to have boyfriends. But in the old days I was a bit of a ladies' man."

"What, you mean  snogging and all that?" said Charlie, screwing his face up. "Yuk!"

"Yeah," Zeus said, nodding. His face went a bit dreamy. "You know, I haven't had a big wet snoggy kiss from a pretty mortal in ever such a long time."

Artemis glared at him suspiciously. "Well, you're not starting now!" Then her face took on a superior, know-all kind of look. "Anyway, you wouldn't stand a chance with Miss Wise. She's practically one of my followers already."

"Oh, is that so?" Zeus asked indignantly, snapping out of his daydream. "That's all *you* know! Give me just two days, and I'll bet you anything you like I *could* get a kiss off Miss Wise, so there!"

"Anything?" Artemis said slyly.

"Anything at all!"

"All right, then!" Artemis grinned. It wasn't a nice grin. "You've got till the end of lunch time, two days from now. If you can't get Miss Wise to kiss you by then, you can clear off back to Olympus and I get to turn your High Priest here into a pig!"

Chapter Three

Actaeon

I was expecting Zeus to say no – or at
least hoping he would – but did he?
Fat chance! Instead he grinned right
back and said, "And if I *do*, then *you*
can clear off back to Olympus!"

"Right!" said Artemis.

"Fine!" said Zeus.

"Deal!" said Artemis.

"Done!" said Zeus.

"And no cheating!"
Artemis added.

Zeus looked shocked. "Artykins!" he said. "As if I would!"

"You *know* you would!" Artemis said accusingly. "But it doesn't count if you do. Miss Wise has to kiss you of her own free will. You're not allowed to use magic to make her *think* she wants to kiss you!"

Zeus smirked. "I don't need to!" he said. "I can win without doing magic on her!"

"Good!" said Artemis. "I'll meet you in here at the end of lunch in two days' time. And *I'm* going to win!" She turned on her heel and marched defiantly from the classroom.

I turned on Zeus.

"What did you do *that* for?" I asked.

"There's no pleasing some mortals, is there?" he complained. "I thought you *wanted* me to get rid of her. And when I win, she'll go!"

"But what if you lose?"

He frowned. "I see what you
mean," he said. "That *would* be a
problem." He thought for a
moment, and then snapped his
fingers. "Got it!" he said. "If she *does*
win . . ."

"Yes?" I said.

"Which she won't, of course, because
I'm going to—"

"Yes, but if she *does*?" I said.

"If she *does* win," he said again, "and turns you into a pig . . ."

"Yes?" I said again.

"Then Charlie here can be my High Priest! Problem solved!"

"But what about *me*?" I said.

Zeus rolled his eyes. "You mortals are all the same," he said. "It's all 'me, me, me' with you lot, isn't it? No thought of how it might feel to be a god with no priest. Anyway, it's probably not so bad being a pig. I might try it myself sometime.

Now," he went on, "how am I going to get Miss Wise to kiss me?" He looked around the classroom for inspiration, and his eyes lit on one of the books by the Greek display – *The Bumper Book of Greek Myths*.

"Aha!" he said. "Bound to be some ideas in there!"

"Well, look on the bright side," I said to Charlie as we left the classroom, leaving Zeus leafing through the book and pondering how he was going to get his kiss.

"We've got a Greek god in the classroom who wants to snog our teacher, and another one in the playground who wants to turn you into a pig!" he said. "What's the bright side to that?"

"Things can't possibly get any worse," I told him.

How wrong I was.

We got outside just in time to see Artemis – or Diana – and her followers charging madly across the playground, knocking Troy to the ground. He clutched his knee, furiously blinking away tears.

"I'm going to *get* that Diana," he muttered.

Great. Now, on top of keeping Zeus out of sight and trying to stop Artemis causing any more trouble, we had to stop Troy from doing anything silly and getting himself turned into a hedgehog or something.

Fortunately, at that moment the bell went for lining up.

Miss Wise came out and clapped her hands to get our attention.

"Now, listen everyone," she said. "As you know, first lesson this afternoon is PE, so I'd like you all to get your kit on the way and then quickly come into the classroom to get changed."

"I'm not going to get changed in the classroom," Artemis said haughtily, not bothering to put her hand up. "I don't want the boys seeing me in my pants. I'll go and get changed somewhere private."

All the other girls agreed loudly,

saying that they didn't want the boys seeing their knickers either – as if any of us wanted to! – and that they weren't going to get changed in the classroom.

Normally, Miss Wise would have got really cross at all this shouting out, and especially with anyone saying they weren't going to do what she'd told them. Instead, though, she just looked thoughtful for a moment and then said, "Good point, Diana. All the girls can go and get changed in the cloakroom."

Artemis made a dash for the doors, with the other girls stampeding after

 her, knocking one of the dinner ladies flying.

"Hmmmph," muttered Troy crossly.

"How come *they* never get told off?"

There was no sign of Zeus in the classroom, but the book he'd been reading was open on my table at the start of the story of Perseus. I glanced at it as I got changed.  Apparently Danae, Perseus's mum, had been shut up by her dad in a locked room so she couldn't have any boyfriends or get married, but Zeus had got in disguised as a shower of golden rain. It didn't say how the golden rain had got in – maybe there was a hole in the roof. Come to that, it didn't say how a shower of rain, golden or otherwise, could have given Perseus's mum a big snoggy kiss, but it sounded like the sort of daft thing Zeus would do.

As soon as I was changed, I sat down for a proper look at the book. I wanted to find out more about Artemis, so I checked the contents page. The only myth I could find with her name in the title was 'Artemis and Actaeon', so I looked that one up.

It was a bit horrible, really. This bloke Actaeon was out hunting in the forest, and he came upon a pool in a clearing. It was just his bad luck that Artemis and her followers were having a bath in it.

Artemis got all cross that he'd seen her with no clothes on, which seems a bit unfair to me. I mean, if you don't want anyone to see you with no clothes on, you shouldn't take them off where anyone might just wander past, should you? And it's not as if there was a sign up saying 'DANGER! GRUMPY GODDESS BATHING! KEEP OUT!'

But anyway, then she accused him of wanting to go round telling everyone he'd seen her in the nude – as if he'd done it on purpose – and she turned him into a stag.

That wasn't the worst bit, though. The worst bit was that Actaeon had been hunting deer, and when he turned into a stag his hunting dogs didn't realize it was him. So they chased and killed him.

I felt really sorry for Actaeon after reading that story.

And then, moments later, I felt really worried.

Because, I suddenly noticed, Troy wasn't in the classroom. Which was Very Bad News. I remembered how upset and angry he'd been when he'd muttered, "I'm going to *get* that Diana." Knowing Troy, that meant he was going to try to get his revenge by doing something that he knew she would hate.

But "that Diana" wasn't who she seemed to be. So if I was right, Troy was doing something incredibly dangerous.

He was trying to see the goddess Artemis's knickers.

Chapter Four

Artemis

"Miss Wise," I said, putting my hand up, "where's Troy gone?"

Miss Wise smiled. "Not that it's any of your business, Alex," she said, "but he was the first to get changed, for once, so I sent him to see if the girls are ready yet."

I'd been afraid of that.

"Um . . . would you like me to go and help him?" I said, touching my little thunderbolt. When he'd given it to me Zeus had promised that it would bring me luck, and I thought I'd

46

probably need a bit of luck to stop
Miss Wise saying, "Don't be silly, Alex.
What kind of help could he possibly
need to do a job like that?"

Miss Wise smiled again.
"Don't be silly, Alex," she
said. "What kind of
help could he possibly
need to do a job like
that?"

So much for the
thunderbolt bringing
me luck. I went back to
my place and worried. What would
Artemis do to Troy if she caught him
looking at her pants? He didn't have
any hunting dogs, so she probably
wouldn't turn him into a stag, but
she'd probably do something just as
nasty. Maybe she'd turn him into a
bag of crisps and wait for Charlie to
come by.

And then the classroom door burst open and Troy came in, a bit breathless, as if he'd been running.

"They've got their PE kit on, Miss, but they say they won't come till they're good and ready!" he said.

Miss Wise looked stern. "What a thing to say, Troy! I'm surprised at you, trying to get the girls into trouble like that!"

"But they *did* say that, Miss—!" Troy began.

"Not another word, Troy!" Miss Wise said sharply. "Go and sit down at once!"

Troy stomped angrily back to his seat. "It's not *fair*!" he muttered. "They *did* say that. And they *are* ready, I *saw* them!"

I realized what must have happened. By the time Troy had got to the cloakrooms, they were all in their PE kits already, so he hadn't seen Artemis's pants. Maybe the thunderbolt had brought me luck after all.

"Troy!" I whispered. "Were you trying to see the girls' knickers?"

He nodded. "I'm going to get that Diana back somehow," he said, "and if she doesn't want anyone seeing her pants then I'm going to!"

"You mustn't!" I said. "You'll get . . ."

Troy snorted. ". . . into trouble?" he finished for me.

Actually, I'd been about to say "turned into a bag of crisps", but thinking about it, there was no point in saying that, was there? He'd never believe me.

I nodded. "Yeah," I said, "you'll get into trouble."

He snorted again. "Ever since *she* got here," he said angrily, "I've been getting into trouble anyway. I might as well get into trouble for something I've actually done!"

And then there was the sound of rowdy laughter, and shouting, and stampeding down the corridor – the sort of thing the boys would have got in trouble for almost before it happened – and the classroom door opened with a *bang!*

"Looks like rain," Artemis said to Miss Wise. "You'd better bring your umbrella, just in case. Come on, let's go!"

She turned on her heels
and sprinted away.
Miss Wise smiled
vaguely, picked up her
umbrella, and followed.

It was *supposed* to be indoor PE that
afternoon. We were *supposed* to be
carrying on with the apparatus work
we'd been doing the week before. But
apparently Artemis had decided we
were doing sports outside instead.
Throwing the javelin, to be precise.

Luckily, the only javelins the school
owns are really soft ones, made of
foam. Luckily for the boys,
particularly, because Artemis decided
we should play a hunting game with
each of the girls having a javelin (or
"spear", as she kept saying) and all
the boys being targets. Actually, it
could have been a fun game, except

that they were all so serious about it and laughed in a really mean way if one of us got hit.

And of course Artemis chose me as her target, and no matter how far or fast I ran, or what I hid behind, she always got me with her javelin straight away.

After about twenty minutes of this I went to Miss Wise and complained that being hunted like an animal wasn't meant to be part of our education, but she just said, "Stop moaning, Alex. It's a good game. It's probably in the National Curriculum somewhere." As if that made it OK.

As Artemis biffed me on the head from about a hundred metres away for what seemed like the fiftieth time, I wondered where Zeus was.

And then Artemis turned to Miss Wise and said, "I think it's starting to rain."

"Thank you, Diana," Miss Wise said. She lifted her umbrella – it's one of those ones which open automatically, with a really powerful spring mechanism – and pressed the button. With a mighty *whoomph!* the umbrella shot open just in time to catch the first raindrops.

OW!

Ouch!

There was something odd about this rain, though. In fact,

there were a few odd things about it.
Firstly, it wasn't falling
anywhere except on Miss Wise.
Secondly, it was a shiny,
golden colour; and if you
looked carefully, you could
see it glowing with a
sort of magical light.
And thirdly,
as the raindrops hit
the umbrella,
I could just hear
Zeus's voice under
each pitter-patter,
going "Oooch!
Ouch! Ow!"
Artemis could hear
it, too. I could tell
by the way she was
grinning. Miss Wise, on
the other hand, didn't
seem to notice.

"Goodness, that was a short shower!" she said cheerily, as the last few golden raindrops trickled off the umbrella and landed with a groan on the hard black playground.

"There might be more, though," Artemis said. "Let's go in now."

And without waiting for permission, she and the other girls ran inside, yelling and screaming. The boys all stared miserably after them. We knew that if we tried running in like that we'd get into huge trouble; but with Artemis around, the girls seemed to be allowed to do whatever they liked.

"Alex and Troy," Miss Wise said, "I'd like you to collect up all the javelins and put them away, please." And she led the rest of the boys inside.

While Troy was stomping around at the other end of the playground, picking up javelins and muttering to himself, I knelt down where Miss Wise had been standing. I could see little golden droplets sparkling on the tarmac.

"Zeus," I said quietly, "are you OK?"

The little golden droplets groaned and began to trickle together. As they did, they turned into a hamster. When Zeus had been here before, he'd disguised himself as a hamster so my parents wouldn't know I had a Greek god in my room.

The hamster sat up and rubbed himself wearily.

"Owww!" he groaned. "That umbrella really hurt when it shot up like that! I've got bruises all over! She's such a *cheat*, that Artemis."

"She's a menace," I agreed. "And on top of everything else, now we've got to stop Troy from seeing her pants. I bet as soon as we've gathered the javelins up he'll sneak in and try to take a look while she's changing."

"Oooh," said Zeus, "she *hates* that. She'll go mad!"

"That's why we've got to stop him from doing it!" I said. "She'll probably turn him into somebody's lunch!"

Zeus rubbed his bruises a bit more and looked sorry for himself.

"It's not my problem," he said sulkily. "Why should *I* help?"

I thought fast. "Because she'd probably enjoy catching him and turning him into something," I said. "And why should she have the fun of doing that, after she told Miss Wise to put her umbrella up?"

Zeus scowled a little hamstery scowl.

"Good point," he said, waving a paw.
A wind sprang up and blew the
javelins Troy was holding out of his
arms, so that he had to chase after
them. "That should
keep him busy until
they've finished
changing," he
said, scuttling up
my arm and
onto my
shoulder, where
he changed into
some kind of
beetle and hid in
my ear.

Zeus was right – by the time we'd
finished tidying up and come in, all
the girls were changed and running
about in the corridors.

The rest of the afternoon went by
relatively calmly, but I couldn't relax.

I hoped Zeus was going to get Miss Wise to kiss him soon.

Tomorrow, to be precise. Because if Zeus hadn't got his kiss by the end of lunch time on the day after that, I was going to be eating swill and saying "oink" for the rest of my life.

Chapter Five

Europa

The next morning
Zeus was in a
determined mood
as he hid himself in
my ear, disguised
as a beetle.

"I'm going to get
that kiss today," he told me
as we got to school. "Let's get that
Bumper Book of Greek Myths and search
for inspiration!"

We had a few minutes' reading time
after play that morning, so I opened
the book up at the contents page and
pretty soon Zeus found exactly what
he was looking for.

"Europa!" he said. "Of course! That's all the inspiration I need! Just give me a couple of minutes, Alex, and I'll have the perfect plan all sorted out!"

While Zeus sat in my ear, working on his idea and mumbling to himself about the details, I read the story. It was a bit of a weird one. Apparently, Zeus fancied this princess called Europa, and, rather than just sending her flowers or asking her out, he turned himself into a beautiful white bull.

Which seems stupid to me. I mean, what if some of the priests had seen him? Wouldn't it be really embarrassing for a god to be sacrificed to himself by his own priests? Imagine ending up as roast bull in your own temple!

But for whatever reason, Zeus decided that if he was going to stand

a chance of going out with Europa,
he ought to be a bull. So he turned
up, in disguise, when she was at the
beach. At the beach! Wouldn't a crab
or a jellyfish have made more sense?
How many bulls do you see at the
seaside?

Anyway, then he just sort of hung
around looking tame, until she
decided to sit on his back. Which
seems the daftest bit of all to me.

I reckon you'd have to be pretty dim to go round sitting on strange bulls. But as soon as she did that, he jumped up and galloped over the sea to another country, where he told her who he was and she decided to go out with him.

Maybe those ancient Greek women were different from nowadays. But I can't imagine any of the grown-ups I know falling in love with someone just because he disguises himself as a farm animal and kidnaps her. Not Miss Wise, certainly; and I told Zeus so.

"Don't you worry, kiddo," he said.

"Leave it to me; I'll save your bacon. Ha! Get it? Bacon!"

I hoped he was right. He certainly wasn't funny.

It was our swimming lesson that day, and after lunch we went to the pool.

As we went into the changing rooms, I noticed Zeus wasn't in my ear any more. Since he'd spent the whole morning boasting about how he was going to save me, but hadn't come up with a single idea, I wasn't too bothered.

That was because I didn't know what he was planning.

All of us started to get changed, except for Troy, who checked the whole wall to see if there was a hole through which he could see the girls. There wasn't.

About five minutes later, just as I'd finished getting changed, there was a scream from the pool area. All the boys ran for the door to see what was happening, except for Troy, who'd just taken his trousers off.

He started yelling, "Oi! Close the door, you lot!"

I think he was worried one of the girls would look in and see *his* pants, but right then no one was interested in anything but who had screamed – and why.

Most of the others got to the door before Charlie and me, and by the time we reached the poolside almost everyone was there, staring and pointing at the pool and talking loudly.

Sophie was in tears – she'd been the one who'd come in first and screamed – and Hélène was giggling.

Charlie and I looked at each other and groaned, "Oh, *no*!"

There, sitting in the shallow end, staring at Miss Wise with the *soppiest* expression on its face, was a huge white bull with a beautiful golden ring in its nose.

The bull mooed softly.

"I don't reckon hearing those stories about himself is good for him," Charlie whispered to me. "It gives him funny ideas."

I reckoned Charlie was right.

"All right, everyone, *be quiet*!" Miss Wise said – not too loudly or crossly, but amazingly everyone shut up at once. She moved to the poolside – just by the big wide steps that go down into the water – and knelt down. The bull stood up and waded towards her. Some of the other kids gasped.

I didn't think Miss Wise was going to be daft enough to sit on Zeus's back. I wasn't sure what he was planning to do if she did, though – I mean, galloping across the sea to another country is one thing, but galloping across the swimming pool to the footbath? Not very romantic, really.

 I looked at Artemis. She looked a bit worried. She stepped forward and cleared her throat, but before she could say anything Miss Wise looked round.

"Quiet, everyone!" she warned. "Not a sound! We don't want to scare him!"

The bull looked warningly at Artemis, and a tiny flash of lightning leaped between his horns. One or two of the kids stared, not quite believing what they'd seen.

"He wants to be careful doing that," Charlie whispered. "He'll electrocute himself if the lightning gets in the water!"

Artemis closed her mouth sulkily.

The bull turned back towards Miss Wise, and the soppy look came into his eyes again. He mooed ever so softly, and put one hoof on the bottom step. Sophie let out a little scream and put her hand to her mouth, but Miss Wise calmly stood up and stepped gently back, giving the bull room to slowly and clumsily climb out of the pool.

And then, still looking soppily at Miss Wise, Zeus knelt down at her feet.

It went completely quiet. No one made a sound as Miss Wise leaned down and stroked Zeus's nose.

I couldn't move. I watched, hardly daring to breathe. Part of me was a bit worried Miss Wise would be silly enough to get on Zeus's back after all; I mean – apart from the last couple of days, which wasn't really her fault – she was the best teacher I'd ever had, and I didn't want her to end up carried across the sea to a far-off country. Besides which, it would be really difficult to explain that to the head teacher.

But part of me was suddenly very hopeful. All Miss Wise needed to do now was give Zeus one little kiss, and my troubles would be over. Just one little kiss.

Instead, she took hold of the golden ring in Zeus's nose and gently pulled.

The bull let out a little bellow of surprise and got to his feet, his hooves clattering on the tiled floor.

"That's right, up you get," Miss Wise said soothingly. "This way." The bull stopped for a moment, but another gentle tug on the nose-ring and he followed again.

"Girls," Miss Wise said, "we'll have to put him in your changing room until we can find out who owns him, so—"

"Why ours, Miss?" Sophie asked huffily. "Why can't he go in the boys'?"

"Because, Sophie," Miss Wise explained patiently, "the door to the girls' is right in front of him. See? Now, I'd like you to quickly and quietly get all your belongings from the changing room and bring them out here."

They did. All the girls – including Artemis, who was now smirking smugly – quickly scooped up their bags and clothes and carried them out to the poolside. Then, as soon as everything was out of there, Miss Wise led Zeus in and, before he could turn round, quickly stepped out and closed the door behind her.

Suddenly everyone was talking at once.

"Miss, that was *amazing* . . ."

"How did you *do* that?"

"Where did it come from?"

Miss Wise held up her hands for silence.

"All right, all right," she said. "My parents are farmers; I grew up on a farm, so I know how to handle a bull."

"But how did you *do* it? How did you get him to just follow you like that?" someone asked.

"Well," Miss Wise answered, "a bull's nose is very sensitive. If you pull on the ring and he doesn't follow, it's a bit sore and he doesn't like it. So if you're careful, then once you're holding the ring you can get him to go wherever you want. Now, we've lost half the lesson dealing with our visitor – so

74

let's work out how to get everyone who isn't already changed into their swimming costume, and then you can get into the pool."

"I'm not going in there," sniffed Sophie. "He might have done a poo in the water!"

"I hadn't thought of that," Miss Wise admitted. "OK – boys, back in your changing room and get dressed; girls, you'll have to dress out here."

The girls all put their clothes down on the benches around the pool – Artemis put hers down next to me, making piggy grunting noises and grinning nastily. Then they stood, hands on hips, waiting for us to go back into our changing room.

oink oink

All the time we were changing, Troy kept trying to sneak a look outside to see if he could see Artemis in her pants, but Miss Wise was standing guard at the door and he didn't stand a chance.

I was a bit annoyed that Zeus had spoiled our swimming lesson. The way things were looking, it would have been my last one before I was turned into a pig, and I'd have liked the chance to enjoy it.

I was also a little worried that he might still be stuck in the changing room. When I got home that afternoon, though, Zeus was sitting on my bed, one hand clutching his nose. He looked miserable, so I got out a bag of crisps and the old, battered model temple that I kept in my sock drawer. Putting the temple on my head, I began.

"O great and mighty Zeus, I sacrifice this bag of roast-bull-flavour crisps to you—"

"You can stop right now if you want," Zeus grumbled. "I can't smell a thing. Ooh, that *woman*!" He took his hand away from his face. "Look what she did!" he moaned. His nose was bright red and about twice its normal size.

I went to the kitchen and fetched a bag of frozen peas from the freezer.

"Hold this on it," I told him. "It'll help."

"My poor nose!" he moaned, pressing the peas against it. "Your teacher's a monster! I've half a mind to smite her!"

"Don't do that," I said. "She'll never kiss you if you do, and then Artemis wins the bet."

"I don't understand," he complained. "What did I do wrong? It worked with Europa."

"Times have changed," I told him. "Maybe in ancient Greece you could impress a woman by turning into a bull and kidnapping her, but nowadays people don't do that."

"What *do* they do?" he asked.

"Well – I think they ask each other out. You know, to the pictures, or out for dinner or something, and they get to know each other. And then they decide if they want to go out properly."

Zeus thought about this.

"It's more fun changing into a bull," he said.

Chapter Six

Pig Day

I woke up early the
next morning
feeling really
worried. It took
me a couple of
moments before I
remembered why.

It was Pig Day. Unless Zeus managed
to get a kiss off Miss Wise by the end of
lunch time, the goddess Artemis was
going to turn me into a pig.

Zeus, of course, was all smiles.

"Not to worry," he said, "we'll take
another look at *The Bumper Book of
Greek Myths*. There's bound to be
something in there."

"What's the use, Zeus?" I asked miserably. "Nothing's worked so far."

Zeus grinned. "I'll think of something," he said.

But he didn't. By the time I set off for school Zeus hadn't had a single idea. Not one. I gave Mum and Dad an extra hug – just in case it was the last chance I got.

We arrived at school a few minutes early and went straight to the classroom, where I opened *The Bumper Book* up at the contents page and read out all the titles. Zeus – sitting on the table in his hamster shape – stopped me every time I got to the name of one of his old girlfriends.

"Leda!" he said. "She was one. I turned into a white swan to get her attention."

"Turning into things hasn't been very successful so far," I reminded him. "You turned into golden rain and Miss Wise biffed you with her umbrella. You turned into a bull and she stretched your nose. If you turn into a swan, she'll probably have you stuffed and roasted for Sunday lunch."

"Fair point," he agreed. "Keep going."

I did. The very next name made him sit up and grin a little hamsterish grin.

"Io!" he said. "She was nice!"

"What happened with her?" I asked.

He chuckled. "It was quite funny, really," he said. "I had to turn her into a cow."

"That's not much use," I said. "I can't see Miss Wise wanting to kiss you if you turn her into a cow."

"No," he said. "Anyway, I did that *after* I kissed her . . . but it's a long story. Keep going."

I did.

"Callisto!" he said a moment later. "She was another one!"

"What did you turn her into, then?" I asked.

"Oh, I didn't turn her into anything," he said.

"That sounds more promising."

"Not really. *I* didn't turn her into anything, but Artemis did. She turned her into a bear. Callisto was one of her followers, you see, so she wasn't supposed to have a boyfriend."

"Oh," I said. "Not much help, then."

"Not really, no."

I carried on down the contents page

until I got to Semele.

"Oh, yes," Zeus said, "she was one of my girlfriends, too."

"And what did she get turned into?" I asked.

"She didn't get turned into anything. She got all burned up."

I closed the book with a sigh. "This isn't really helping, is it?" I asked.

He rolled his eyes. "You're such a Walter Worrywart!" he said.

"It's all right for you," I told him. "If someone turned you into a pig, you could just turn yourself back again." I stood up sadly. "I suppose we'd better get outside. The bell will be ringing in a minute."

Suddenly, Zeus snapped his fingers. "Hang on!" he said. "Alcmene!"

"What?" I said.

"Alcmene!" he said again. "How could I forget? I got to kiss her by using a foolproof trick! Absolutely one hundred per cent foolproof!"

I stared at him. "Really?" I said. "It's guaranteed to work?"

"Completely guaranteed!" he said. "I've used the same trick loads of times and it's never failed. It just can't!"

"Great!" I said, all excited. "What did you do?"

"It's really simple," he smiled. "I disguised myself as her husband!"

My heart sank.

"Zeus," I said, "Miss Wise doesn't *have* a husband. She doesn't even have a boyfriend. That's the whole point, remember? That's why Artemis wants her as a follower!"

And then the bell went and I had to rush outside and line up.

To give Zeus credit, he didn't stop trying all morning. In fact, he tried all kinds of things. For instance, he tried turning into a beautiful white dove and flying in through the window.

Unfortunately, Miss Wise had just shut the window. He went straight into it.

He tried turning into a sweet little cat who came into the classroom and jumped up on her desk.

How was he to know Miss Wise is allergic to cats? She sneezed so hard she almost blew him back out of the door again.

He tried turning into a cup of coffee. That was quite clever, actually – Miss Wise loves coffee. Sadly, she spent playtime marking our homework and he went cold. Then, as luck would have it, one of the other teachers came in and collected all the coffee mugs from her desk – there were about twelve – so he ended up being emptied out, washed up, and used for the head teacher's horrible herbal tea.

He even disguised himself as Mr Cameron, the schoolkeeper, and tried getting a kiss from her that way. She slapped him round the face.

So it was that after lunch, when I should have been outside playing and having fun, I was spending my last few minutes as a human boy sitting gloomily in the classroom with Charlie and a talking hamster.

"The shame!" Zeus was saying. "How am I going to live it down! It'll be all round Olympus by sunset that I lost a bet with my own daughter!"

"You'll get over it," I said unsympathetically. "Whereas I won't."

"You might!" Zeus argued.

I glared at him. "How, exactly, might I ever get over being a pig?" I asked.

"Well – you might get over not *enjoying* being a pig," he said. "And I don't know what *you're* so miserable about," he added, looking at Charlie.

"I'm about to lose my best friend!" Charlie pointed out.

"You're not going to *lose* him," Zeus said. "He'll still be here – he'll just be a different shape! And if you ever stop being friends with him, you can have him for lunch! Mmmm – crispy bacon sandwiches! Lovely! You could even sacrifice him to me first!"

And then, just when I thought nothing
worse could happen, the door behind
us opened and Miss Wise said, "Alex!
Charlie! What are you doing inside?"

Great. Only a few minutes to go
before I got turned into a pig, and I
was going to spend those last precious
minutes being told off. And to make
matters worse – she'd seen Zeus.

"Boys," she said, "you both know you're not even supposed to bring toys to school, never mind pets!" She strode into the room and without giving us time to say anything, she scooped him up. "Whose is he?" she demanded.

I thought I might as well take the blame. I mean, she could hardly keep a pig in at playtime, could she? "He's mine," I said. "His name's Zeus."

"Well, what a silly thing to do, Alex," she said. "Letting him loose inside the classroom. Anything might happen to him. He might get lost! Mr Cameron's cat might get him!" She looked at me sternly. "You wouldn't want that to happen, would you?"

"No, Miss Wise," I said quietly, although at that moment the idea of Zeus being eaten by a cat had a certain appeal.

"No, you wouldn't," Miss Wise told

me, stroking Zeus's furry back gently with one finger. "Really, Alex! I'd have thought you'd be more sensible!" She looked at Zeus, holding him up as she did so. "I'm sure you'd be really sad if anything happened to him. He's such a sweet little thing."

And then, quite unexpectedly, still stroking his back, she leaned forward and gently kissed his little pink nose.

"Put him away safely and then come straight out!" she added, handing him carefully to me. And with that, she was gone.

Chapter Seven

Underwear of the Gods

Charlie and I stared at Zeus. He stared back.

"Wa-*hoooo*!" he suddenly yelled, leaping off my hand and landing on the floor in front of me. He did a funny little wiggly dance, both front paws waving excitedly in the air. "Yes!" he shouted. "Yes, yes, *yes*! I'm the greatest! I'm the best! *I did it!*"

And then Charlie and I were dancing, too, with sheer delight and relief that I wasn't going to be turned into a pig after all; and somewhere in the middle of all this Zeus turned back into his own shape, and we were all laughing and cheering and high-fiving . . .

And then the door opened again,
and Artemis came in.

"Pig time!" she announced cheerily.

"No it isn't!" Zeus told her, wiggling
his bottom happily as he danced
triumphantly round her. "It's time for
you to go back home to Mount
Olympus, that's what time it is!

Because I won! See?" He
pointed at a big red
smudge on the end of
his nose. "See that?
Miss Wise's lipstick,
that's what that is! I
am the winner, you
are the loser, nah nah
nee nah nah!"

Artemis examined the lipstick mark.
"That doesn't count!" she scowled.
"It's just a kiss on the nose, not a big
sloppy snog!"

"We didn't say anything about a big
sloppy snog!" Zeus reminded her. "The
bet was, I'd get a kiss off Miss Wise
before the end of lunch time today,
without having to magic her to do it.
And I did! Bye-bye, sweetie-pie! Off
you go!"

Artemis glared at him. Then she
glared at me.

"This is all your fault," she said. She turned back to Zeus. "Can't I turn him into *something*, Dad?" she whined. "*Pleee*-ease?"

Zeus chuckled and shook his head.

"Yeah, well," Artemis grumbled sulkily, glaring at me again, "I'll teach you. You don't mess around with me and get away with it!" And before I could say anything, there was a bright flash and where Charlie had been a moment earlier there was suddenly a very startled-looking pig.

I was outraged. "You can't do that!" I said. "That's cheating!"

"*How* is it cheating, then?" Artemis crowed. "I'm not allowed to turn *you* into a pig. I never said anything about your daft friend. That'll teach you, won't it?"

"But . . . but . . . it's not *fair*!" I said. I turned to Zeus. "Tell her she can't do that!" I demanded. "Make her change him back!"

He shrugged. "Nothing to do with me," he said.

"Oink!" said the pig. He trotted off to Miss Wise's desk and tried to get his head into the drawer where she keeps her emergency chocolate.

"Change him *back*!" I said to Artemis.

"Shan't!" she jeered. "Make me!"

"Change him back!" I insisted. "Or . . . or . . . or I'll tell everyone that I saw you in your pants!"

"Yeah, but you didn't, did you?" she said.

"Didn't I?" I asked. "How else would I know what colour they are? They're

 navy blue with little silver bows and arrows all over!"

Artemis gasped. Her hand went to her mouth.

"*Please*, Dad!" she said. "He's just *asking* to be turned into something."

Zeus shook his head. "He's my High Priest, sweetie, and anyway, you lost the bet. Alex is off limits to you!"

"But he's seen me in my pants!"

"Doesn't matter," Zeus said. "He's still off limits. I'd change Charlie back if I were you, Artykins."

Artemis scowled. She growled. She bared her teeth. "Aaaargh!" she howled in frustration. "All *right*!"

97

"Ow!" came Charlie's voice from inside the desk. "Help!" I had to go round and open the drawer a bit wider so he could get his head out. He emerged, looking a bit guilty, with smears of chocolate round his mouth.

"Right," I said to Artemis, "your choice. I'll keep quiet about your pants, if you promise to leave my friends and family alone. But if you do *anything* unkind to *anyone* I know, I'll tell everyone."

She scowled the scowliest scowl I'd ever seen.

"All right!" she growled. "You don't tell anyone else, and I promise I'll leave your friends and family alone. OK?"

Something about the way she said it made me suspicious.

"Not *just* my friends and family," I reminded her. "Everyone I know — Miss Wise, the dinner ladies, *everyone* I know!"

She glared at me. "That's asking a
bit much, isn't it?"

"Not if you don't want the whole
world to find out," I said. "I could set
up a website –
www.artemisinherpants.com!"

She went pale. "No!" she said.
"Promise you won't do that!"

"I promise I won't," I told her, "as
long as you never do anything unkind
to anyone I know."

"All right! All right! I'll leave everyone you know alone!" she snapped. "Happy now?"

"Not quite," I told her. "There's one more thing."

She glared. If looks could turn people into pigs, I'd have been snuffling around in Miss Wise's chocolate drawer just seconds later.

"What?" she growled.

"I want our school back the way it was," I told her. "No more Miss Wise being unfair to the boys. No more gangs of girls terrorizing us at playtime. Do that, and I'll keep quiet about the pants."

"All *right*!" she snarled, and snapped her fingers. "There! Everything's back just how it was.

100

They won't even remember I was here. Will *that* do?"

I nodded.

And then she stamped her foot angrily, and was gone. Just like that.

Charlie stared at me, open-mouthed. "How did you do that?" he said. "That was amazing!"

"It wasn't that clever!" Zeus said. "Not as clever as me getting a kiss off Miss Wise!"

"There wasn't anything clever about that," I reminded him. "She just came in and kissed you when you weren't expecting it."

"Yeah, well," Zeus said, "that means I did it without even trying. That's *really* clever."

"Except when you *did* try, you didn't get anywhere," Charlie pointed out. "But, Alex – when *did* you see Artemis in her pants?"

"Promise not to tell?" I said. Charlie nodded. After a moment, Zeus did, too. "Well . . ." I confessed, "I didn't."

"What?" Charlie burst out.

"I didn't actually lie to her," I pointed out. "I never said I *had* seen her getting changed – just that I'd tell everyone I had. But yesterday, when the girls had to bring their clothes out of the changing room at the pool . . . well, her pants were just sitting on top of her pile of clothes, where anyone could have seen them."

Zeus fell about laughing. And Charlie and I joined in.

We were still roaring with laughter, all three of us, when a sudden thought occurred to me.

"Zeus," I said, "don't you think it's a bit of a coincidence, Artemis turning up in a school you visited only a few weeks ago?"

"Not at all!" he said. "It's probably because I told all the other gods what a great time I had here!"

Zeus seemed to have forgotten that his last visit had ended with him complaining he was bored. But that wasn't what was worrying me.

"Zeus," I said, "are you telling me that at any time we could have another Greek god turning up here and causing trouble?"

"Yes," he grinned, "you probably will. But don't worry; you can always call me to come and help out!"

"But . . ." I began, thinking of how much worse he'd nearly made things this time. "But . . ."

Zeus grinned. "Don't worry," he said, as the bell rang for the end of lunch time. "It's no trouble."

"But . . ." I said again.

"Anyway," he said, "I can't hang around. I've got to get back to Mount Olympus and tell everyone how I won the bet, before Artemis starts making up fibs about it. See you next time!"

And just like that, he was gone, too.

THE END